He whom shepherds once came praising,

Awed by heav'nly light ablazing,

Cheered by angel news amazing:

"King of glory, Christ is born!"

The Shepherd's Christmas Story

Written by Dandi Daley Mackall

Illustrated by Dominic Catalano

CONCORDIA PUBLISHING HOUSE • SAINT LOUIS

Published by Concordia Publishing House
3558 S. Jefferson Avenue, St. Louis, MO 63118-3968
1-800-325-3040 • www.cph.org
Text copyright © 2005 by Dandi Daley Mackall
Illustrations copyright © 2005 by Concordia Publishing House

Manufactured in China

1 2 3 4 5 6 7 8 9 10   14 13 12 11 10 09 08 07 06 05

Were I more than an uneducated shepherd, I would have recorded my every memory of that night. But I could neither read nor write. And perhaps that made it even more amazing that of all the people on earth—kings, nobles, religious leaders, rabbis—the message came to us on that first Christmas.

He came to us.

He could have come to kings

    —with the *ta-ta-DA, ta-ta-DA* of trumpets blaring...

    Not to poor shepherds on a wind-swept hill outside Bethlehem.

    Yet I remember the **whoo-oo whoosh** of the wind on that night.

    The stars shone down on our flocks, bright as a promise.

He could have come to nobles, who kept their distance from us shepherds, as they streamed into Bethlehem to be counted for Quirinius's census.

"Do not worry that they look down on us," said my father, not for the first time. "On these hills, King David sang to his sheep."

"Father Abraham himself was a shepherd," my uncle added.

I listed other shepherds: "And Abel, Rebekah, Jacob, Joseph, Moses, Saul."

"It is an honorable life," my father concluded. "Did not the prophet Ezekiel call God 'Our Shepherd'?"

He could have come at the call of temple priests.

But I remember the call of shepherds as we settled our sheep into the sheepfold. Our sheep know our voices. They follow us. We do not drive them, but lead them to quiet streams and green pastures, as David sang in the psalms.

He could have come in clouds of holy temple fires.

But I remember our small bramble fires on the
hillside as we warmed ourselves. I pulled my camel-hair
cloak around me, lifting the veil against the night wind.
My eyes longed to close. But if I failed to keep watch,
wild beasts waited to attack my sheep. I felt my slingshot
in my pouch, my rod, and my staff. We guarded our sheep
with our lives.

The visit could have come to Herod's grand palace outside the city, surrounded by gold and marble.

But I remember the rocks, sparse grass, and barren olive trees. How it all changed in an instant! An angel appeared among us with the glow of a thousand dawning lights. I dropped to the ground in fear. Around me sounded the *thud, thud, thud* of shepherds' knees bowing before the glory of the Lord.

The angel could have spoken to religious leaders trained to understand revelations.

But he spoke to us:

"Do not be afraid. I bring you good news of great joy that will be for all the people."

The word *all* echoed through the hills. It meant even the lowliest, even the shepherds, even *us*.

And there was more: "Today, in the town of David, a Savior has been born to you; He is Christ the Lord."

Christ the Lord.

Born to us...

To us.

Wiser men might have known how to recognize
this Savior. But the angel understood our ignorance.
"This will be a sign to you: You will find a baby wrapped
in strips of cloth and lying in a manger."

The angel music could have come to temple singers, trained to join in.

But the heavens ripped open before our eyes, and an army of angels descended with the music of the spheres. The hills were ablaze with angel light and song:

"Glory to God in the highest heaven,

And peace on earth to all whom God favors."

The song echoed in our hearts:

...to *all*.

...to *all*.

...to *us!*

And then the angels were gone—slipped behind the veil of heaven, leaving stars as shadows of their glory.

And there was no one but us.

Silence was broken by the voices of my elders. "Let's go to Bethlehem and see this thing that has happened, which the Lord has told us about."

Told *us!*

Told *us!*

The announcement by angels could have been followed by bells *ring-ringing*.

But I remember the *slip-slap* of sandals as we raced, stumbling and laughing, to Bethlehem.

Past the Roman guards at the gate—

Past inns and travelers—

Flip flap

Slip slap

The angels told us

...Told us!

The Savior could have been born in the Temple of Jerusalem, where we take our best, our perfect lambs for sacrifice. The aroma of incense would have blessed the air.

But I remember the smell of hay mixed with donkey sweat and cows. And there, in the manger, was a child, small and wrapped in strips of cloth—

The Lamb of God

Come to *us!*

The greeting to Mary and Joseph could have come from rabbis, their words clear and filled with learning.

But as we repeated all the angels had said, our words tumbled from us like sheep diving off a cliff. Joseph stared at us, as if trying to grasp each word. But Mary held her child and smiled. It was as if our words sank into her and stayed.

The good news could have been carried from the stable to kings and queens, nobles and warriors.

But I remember our joyful shouts as we shared all we had heard and seen—

...to the late night travelers,

...to the early morning breadmakers,

...to the Roman guards at the gate.

Then we returned to the hills outside Bethlehem. And we glorified God, the Great Shepherd, who had sent such good news—

—to *us*

—to *us*

—to *us!*

$\mathcal{J}$esus visited many during His stay on earth. He told a story about searching for one lost sheep.

He said, "I am the Good Shepherd. The Good Shepherd lays down His life for His sheep." Then He became our Lamb of Sacrifice, dying for our sins. When He rose again, He told His friend, Peter, "Feed My sheep."

I believe our Savior never forgot us shepherds.

We shall never forget Him.

The wond'ring shepherds said: "Behold!

Let us now go with all good speed to Bethlehem
To see this thing the Lord has told;
The sheep are safe; he will indeed take care of them."

There they found the wonder child, in lowly swaddling clothes lying,
Yet all the world with his free grace supplying.

God's own Son is born a child, is born a child;
God the Father is reconciled, is reconciled!